WRITTEN & ILLUSTRATED BY BOB FULLER

MEET THE KIDS OF
Paddywhack Lane

✤ A STORY ABOUT FRIENDSHIP ✤

GROSSET & DUNLAP /  WALDEN MEDIA

GROSSET & DUNLAP
Published by the Penguin Group
Penguin Group (USA) Inc., 375 Hudson Street, New York, New York 10014, U.S.A.
Penguin Group (Canada), 90 Eglinton Avenue East, Suite 700, Toronto, Ontario, Canada M4P 2Y3
(a division of Pearson Penguin Canada Inc.)
Penguin Books Ltd, 80 Strand, London WC2R 0RL, England
Penguin Ireland, 25 St Stephens Green, Dublin 2, Ireland
(a division of Penguin Books Ltd)
Penguin Group (Australia), 250 Camberwell Road, Camberwell, Victoria 3124, Australia
(a division of Pearson Australia Group Pty Ltd)
Penguin Books India Pvt Ltd, 11 Community Centre, Panchsheel Park, New Delhi - 110 017, India
Penguin Group (NZ), Cnr Airborne and Rosedale Roads, Albany, Auckland 1310, New Zealand
(a division of Pearson New Zealand Ltd)
Penguin Books (South Africa) (Pty) Ltd, 24 Sturdee Avenue, Rosebank, Johannesburg 2196, South Africa

Penguin Books Ltd, Registered Offices:
80 Strand, London WC2R 0RL, England

This book is published in partnership with Walden Media, LLC. Walden Media and
the Walden Media skipping stone logo are trademarks and registered trademarks of
Walden Media, LLC, 294 Washington Street, Boston, Massachusetts 02108.

www.paddywhacklane.com

Library of Congress Control Number: 2006018333

ISBN 978-0-448-44508-3   10 9 8 7 6 5 4 3 2 1

Joshua, Rachel, Benjamin, Lauren, Courtney, Kayla, Lindsay, and Jacob Parker had just moved into a new house on Paddywhack Lane with their parents and their pets—Oliver the puppy and Fluff the kitty.

The kids couldn't wait to make some new friends in the neighborhood.

Josh spotted a boy and girl next door.

"Come on," Josh called to his brother and sister. "Let's see if those kids want to play with us."

"Hi! I'm Josh, and this is my brother Jacob and my sister Kayla. We just moved in next door."

The boy looked up. "I'm Anthony, and she's Madeline."

"Do you want to come over and play?" Kayla asked.

Madeline sighed. "Not really."

"Curtis and Sylvia used to live in your house,
but they moved away," Anthony added.

"Well, never mind," Kayla said, pretending like it didn't bother her.

"Yeah," Jacob added, "we actually need to get home. See you later."

"I guess they're just not interested in making new friends," Kayla said as they walked away.

"Don't worry," Josh said. "I'm sure there are plenty more kids to meet around here."

Kayla, Josh, and Jacob walked back home. Rachel and Courtney were sitting on the steps, looking bored.

"Why don't we all take a walk to see if we can find some other kids to play with?" Josh suggested.

They hadn't walked very far when they saw a girl and a boy, working in their garden.

"That sure is a beautiful garden!" Rachel said to the girl.
"I'm Rachel, and these are my brothers and sisters," she continued.

"I'm Jade, and this is my brother Daniel," the girl said.

"Do you need some help with your garden?" Rachel asked.

"Thanks, but we can manage by ourselves," Daniel replied.

"Well, if you ever want to play sometime, we live down the street," Josh said.

The kids left Jade and Daniel and continued down the block, looking for some kids to meet.

"There's Benjamin and Lindsay!" Courtney called out.

"Come and see what I invented!" Benjamin shouted.

His brothers and sisters ran over.

"Where did you get that kite?" Courtney asked Benjamin.

"From Sophia and Emily," Benjamin replied, pointing to the two girls walking toward them.

"Our kite was caught in a tree, but we met Benjamin and he climbed up and rescued it," Sophia said.

"Then he showed us his trick of using thread instead of heavy string to fly the kite," Emily added.

"Cool!" Josh said. "We just moved in down the street, and we were wondering if you would like to come…"

"Oh, no!" the girls cried out before they had a chance to answer.

Everyone ran over to Benjamin.

"Don't worry," Benjamin said. "I just have to give the kite a little tug."

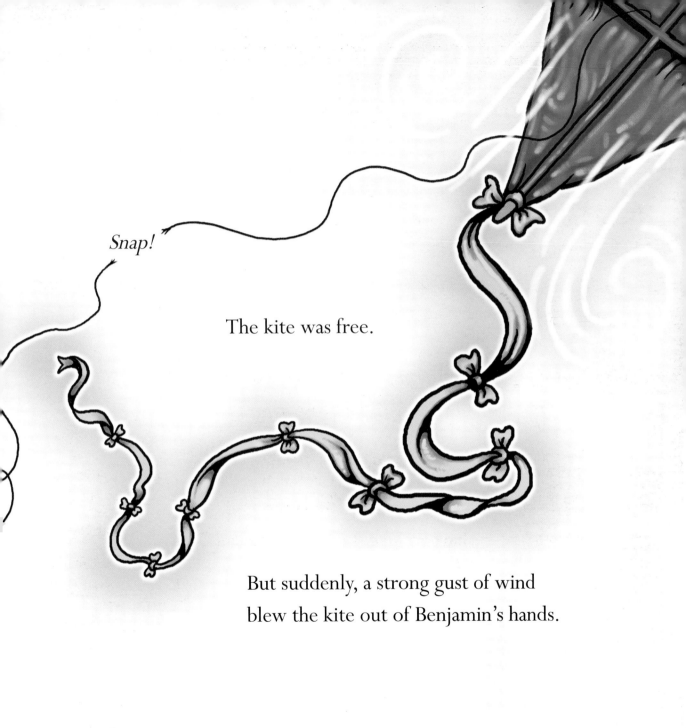

Snap!

The kite was free.

But suddenly, a strong gust of wind
blew the kite out of Benjamin's hands.

"Our kite!" Sophia yelled. "Look what you've done."

And with that, the girls ran off.

"This friend-finding stuff is hard work," Josh said.

"Come on," said Lindsay, "let's go home and play by ourselves!"

But once they got home, the kids couldn't think of anything to do.

"Check out what Josh drew!" Benjamin said.

"That's an amazing picture," Lauren said. "You look so cute in that puppy costume."

"I have an idea," Rachel said. "Let's all draw pictures of ourselves wearing costumes. I know exactly what I want to be."

Soon everyone had finished their drawings.

Benjamin drew himself in a bear costume.

Rachel made a fluffy rabbit.

Jacob drew a lion with whiskers.

"Wouldn't it be great if we could really have these costumes?" Kayla suggested.

Lauren had an idea. "Maybe we can!"

"Mom did it!" Lauren said a few days later. "She made costumes for all of us! But she said there's one thing we need to remember," Lauren continued. "Dress-up is great fun, but it's what you believe inside that makes you *you*. The outside's mostly fabrics and stitching."

Quickly, the kids tried on their costumes.

"Hey, everybody, let's have a costume parade," Josh suggested.

"That's a great idea!" Rachel agreed. Then they ran outside to play.

Soon, the Parker kids were marching around the neighborhood in a costume parade.

Anthony and Madeline saw the parade and decided to follow along. Jade and Daniel put down their garden tools and got in line, too. When Sophia and Emily saw all of the fun, they joined in as well.

The costumes were a big hit, and so were the Parker kids! Now every kid in the neighborhood wanted a costume.

Josh had an idea. He ran into his house. When he came back outside, he was carrying paper and crayons for all of his new friends. And he had some great news, too—Mrs. Parker had agreed to make costumes for everyone!

A few weeks later, an excited group of kids dressed in spectacular costumes gathered on Paddywhack Lane.

"Ahoy, mateys!" called Anthony, adjusting his pirate eye patch.

Madeline's duck suit came with fluffy feathers and a shiny beak.

Jade danced and twirled in her shimmering fuzzy caterpillar suit.

Daniel marched around, leaving huge
dinosaur footprints everywhere he went.

Sophia wore a snail costume with
a special storage compartment.

Emily wore floppy elephant ears
and a bouncy trunk over her nose.

Surrounded by all of the wonderful new friends
they had made, the Parkers were happy.

Paddywhack Lane was really starting to feel like home.

Standing in the middle of the crowd, Josh yelled, "I have one more idea!"

In his most official-sounding voice, he said, "I hereby declare this the Paddywhack Lane Dress-up Club!"

From that day on, every day was a new adventure on Paddywhack Lane!